Hi my name is Tractor Ted.
I live in Tractorland. It is wintertime
and there is snow on the ground.

TED 1

Tractors work well in wintertime.
They help to clear snow from the roads.

Animals' fur grows very thick
in winter to keep them warm.

TED 1

**Horses wear rugs in winter.
It keeps them dry.**

These sheep are so woolly they can't feel the snow on them.

TED 1

The farmer has to feed them lots of food in
the wintertime because there is no grass for them to eat.

Cows stay in barns in winter.

TED 1

The farmer is feeding them some silage.

While the cows are being milked...

...the farmer clears the slurry from the cows barn
with a yard scraper.

The slurry is kept in a big pit.
The digger is emptying the pit.

TED 1

The slurry is loaded into the spreader.

The slurry is being sprayed onto the fields. It is a smelly job.

The slurry can also be put in a tanker.

TED 1

This machine injects it into the ground.

Markets are still open in wintertime. I wonder what the farmers are unloading from their trailers.

They may be cows. Cows come in lots of different colours. There are black ones...

...there are red ones...

...there are white ones...

...and there are brown ones.

TED 1

Tractors come in different colours. There are red ones...

...there are blue ones...

...there are yellow ones...

...and there are green ones.

TED 1

Those aren't cows. Those are sheep at the market.

The man who sells them is called an auctioneer.

Tractors get very muddy and need a good clean.

It is a good time to check that they are working well.

TED 1

The farmer will need to check
that the hitch is working.

Animals are sometimes born in the wintertime. This calf has just been born...

...and these kittens are only a few weeks old.

I hope you enjoyed reading about Tractorland in Wintertime. Bye Bye!
TED 1

TED 1

Do you know what colour these cows are?

Can you remember the jobs that these machines do?

1

2

3

Can you count how many cows there are?

TED 1